This edition is
published and distributed
exclusively by
DISCOVERY TOYS
Martinez, CA

Originally published by
Walker Books, Ltd.
London

Printed in Italy

ISBN 0-939979-24-1

On the Farm

Julie Lacome

DISCOVERY TOYS

The dog in the farmhouse
went woof, woof, woof.
The puppies in the farmhouse
went yap, yap, yap.

The cat said, "Meow.
It's too noisy here for me."

quack
quack

peep
peep

peep
peep

peep
peep

honk
honk

The cat ran into the farmyard.
The ducks went quack, quack.
The geese went honk, honk.

The cat said, "Meow.
It's too noisy here for me."

The cat ran to the hen house.
The hens went cluck, cluck, cluck.
The rooster went cock-a-doodle-doo.

The cat said, "Meow.
It's too noisy here for me."

The cat ran to the pigsty.
The pigs went grunt, grunt.
The piglets went oink, oink.

The cat said, "Meow.
It's too noisy here for me."

The cat ran to the stables.
The horse went neigh, neigh.
The donkey went hee-haw.

The cat said, "Meow.
It's too noisy here for me."

The cat ran to the field.
The cow went moooooooo.
The sheep went baaaaaaaaa.
The crows went caw, caw, caw.

The cat said, "Meow.
It's too noisy here for me."

The cat ran on up the hill until
she came to the barn.

The barn was warm and quiet.

"Meow," said the cat.
"It's just right here for us!"

The kittens went purr, purr,
purrrrrrr.